丝织的帐篷

英语经典诗歌选译

［英］雪莱（Percy Shelley）等　著

王纯真　译

东南大学出版社
SOUTHEAST UNIVERSITY PRESS
·南京·

图书在版编目(CIP)数据

丝织的帐篷：英语经典诗歌选译：英汉对照 /（英）雪莱（Percy Shelley）等著；王纯真译 .—南京：东南大学出版社，2017.11

ISBN 978-7-5641-6966-4

Ⅰ.①丝… Ⅱ.①雪… ②王… Ⅲ.①英语诗歌－诗集－世界－英、汉 Ⅳ.①I12

中国版本图书馆 CIP 数据核字（2017）第 243637 号

丝织的帐篷

出版发行	东南大学出版社
出 版 人	江建中
社　　址	南京市四牌楼 2 号（邮编 210096）
印　　刷	江苏扬中印刷有限公司
经　　销	全国各地新华书店
开　　本	880mm × 1230mm　1/32
印　　张	6.75
字　　数	115 千字
版　　次	2017 年 11 月第 1 版　2017 年 11 月第 1 次印刷
书　　号	ISBN 978-7-5641-6966-4
印　　数	1-3000 册
定　　价	35.00 元

译者媒也（代序）

新娘美似花，

掀开盖头看。

媒婆站一旁，

最好是无言。

目录

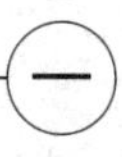
辑

怀 念

风狂雨骤的夜晚

第

爱在迷人的春天

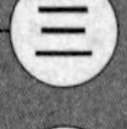

第三辑

太阳落山

第

第一辑

怀念

The Coming Wisdom with Time

William Butler Yeats

扫 码 听 诗

Though leaves are many, the root is one;

Through all the lying days of my youth

I swayed my leaves and flowers in the sun;

Now I may wither into the truth.

时光之悟

[爱尔兰]叶芝(1865—1939)

树叶千千簇,树根孤单单。

在我虚妄的青春岁月里,

绿叶繁花,阳光下摇曳出一片璀璨。

如今叶落花谢,我愿在泥土的纯真里长眠。

To—Music, When Soft Voices Die

Percy Bysshe Shelley

Music, when soft voices die,

Vibrates in the memory—

Odours, when sweet violets sicken,

Live within the sense they quicken.

Rose leaves, when the rose is dead,

Are heaped for the beloved's bed;

And so thy thoughts, when thou art gone,

Love itself shall slumber on.

当轻柔的话语消失

[英]雪莱(1792—1822)

当轻柔的话语消失,

音乐依然在记忆中回旋——

要是紫罗兰发病,

它的香泽依然在感觉中弥漫。

玫瑰凋谢之时,

枯叶堆起,铺成恋人的床单。

等到你辞别人世,

你的思想还在,爱缠绵。

This Living Hand

John Keats

扫 码 听 诗

This living hand, now warm and capable

Of earnest grasping, would, if it were cold

And in the icy silence of the tomb,

So haunt thy days and chill thy dreaming nights

That thou wouldst wish thine own heart dry of blood

So in my veins red life might stream again,

And thou be conscience-calmed—see here it is—

I hold it towards you.

活力迸发的手

［英］济慈（1795—1821）

这活力迸发的手，温暖的手，

渴望抓住命运的缰绳；

假如它冰冷僵硬，

出现在墓穴的死寂之中，

你的白天将困扰着挥之不去的恐惧，

噩梦连连的夜晚变得阴凄鬼冷，

那时节你会情愿让心脏的血液流空。

所以，我的血管里炽热的生命重新启动，

你的心态安详而平静——来，

我把手伸出——握到你的手中。

So We'll Go No More A-Roving

Lord Byron

So, we'll go no more a-roving

So late into the night,

Though the heart be still as loving,

And the moon be still as bright.

For the sword outwears its sheath,

And the soul wears out the breast,

And the heart must pause to breathe,

And love itself have rest.

Though the night was made for loving.

And the day returns too soon,

Yet we'll go no more a-roving

By the light of the moon.

我们再也不用流浪

[英]拜伦(1788—1824)

这么说我们再也不用流浪,

深更半夜在街头彷徨,

虽说这颗心还是充溢着爱意,

月光也还是那样明亮。

剑鞘损毁剑尚在,

身躯消泯,灭不了灵魂,

心总要停止跳动,

爱既开场,也必有剧终。

虽说这夜晚是为爱而生,

白昼又来得过于匆匆,

毕竟,我们再也不用流浪,

去街头欣赏那月光融融。

I Wandered Lonely as a Cloud

William Wordsworth

扫 码 听 诗

I wondered lonely as a cloud

That floats on high o'er vales and hills,

When all at once I saw a crowd,

A host, of golden daffodils;

Beside the lake, beneath the trees,

Fluttering and dancing in the breeze.

Continuous as the stars that shine

And twinkle on the milky way,

They stretched in never-ending line

Along the margin of a bay:

Ten thousand saw I at a glance,

Tossing their heads in sprightly dance.

我像一朵云彩孤独地漫游

[英]华兹华斯(1770—1850)

我孤独地漫游,像一朵云彩,

飘动在高空,飞越万壑千山。

有一次我突然看见

在湖边的树下

一大片金色的水仙,

在微风中轻轻摇曳,舞姿翩翩。

像银河里闪闪发光的星辰,

汇成连绵无尽的一片,

沿着小湾的边缘伸展;

成千上万的花枝,

一下子映入我的眼帘;

摇头晃脑,舞姿翩翩。

The waves beside them danced; but they

Out-did the sparkling waves in glee：

A poet could not but be gay.

In such a jocund company：

I gazed—and gazed—but little thought

What wealth the show to me had brought：

For oft, when on my couch I lie

In vacant or in pensive mood,

They flash upon that inward eye

Which is the bliss of solitude;

And then my heart with pleasure fills,

And dances with the daffodils.

就在它们的身边，浪花也在跳舞，

但它们比浮光跃金的浪花跳得更欢，

有这样快乐的伙伴，真的是

诗人兴会更无前。

我看了又看，但从未想到

这美景会给我带来多少金元。

躺在沙发上，我常常沉思默想，

思绪里泛起一点困惑与茫然，

那一片水仙会在我心灵的眼波里闪现，

是孤寂中的洪福齐天。

那时候，我的心就会溢满欣喜，

跳着，舞着，迎合那一片金色的水仙。

Composed Upon Westminster Bridge

William Wordsworth

Earth has not anything to show more fair!

Dull would he be of soul who could pass by

A sight so touching in its majesty!

This City now doth like a garment wear.

The beauty of the morning: silent, bare.

Ships, towers, domes, theatres, and temples lie

Open unto the fields, and to the sky,

All bright and glittering in the smokeless air.

Never did sun more beautifully steep

In his first splendour, valley, rock, or hill;

Ne’er saw I, never felt, a calm so deep!

The river glideth at his own sweet will:

Dear God! the very houses seem asleep;

And all that mighty heart is lying still!

西敏桥上

[英]华兹华斯

大地之美好真的是无以复加，

谁也不会忽视如此动人的风景，

除非是灵魂呆滞的木头疙瘩：

看城市展现出早晨的明丽，

着一身素装，静谧而娴雅。

船舶，塔楼，穹顶，剧院，礼拜堂

全向着田野和天宇开放；

风物清朗，在明净无烟的空中闪亮。

山谷，岩石，冈峦，

从未曾沐浴过如此壮美的朝阳；

我也从未感受过如此深沉的宁静与安详！

泰晤士河尽情地发着金光：

啊，上帝！华屋茅舍尽在沉睡中，

伟大的造物主也在安歇静养！

The Lost Love

William Wordsworth

She dwelt among the untrodden ways

Beside the springs of Dove;

A maid whom there were none to praise,

And very few to love.

A violet by a mossy stone

Half hidden from the eye!

Fair as a star, when only one

Is shining in the sky.

She lived unknown, and few could know

When Lucy ceased to be;

But she is in her grave, and oh,

The difference to me!

失去的爱

[英]华兹华斯

她住在人迹罕至的地方，

不远处就是那鸽泉。

一个女孩，无人疼爱，

也少有人夸赞。

长满苔藓的岩石旁，

一株紫罗兰，半露半掩，

美得像孤星，

照亮天边。

默默无闻地活着，

谁也不知她何时辞了人间；

她去墓园安息了，

唉，我这里像是天塌地陷。

I Traveled among Unknown Men

William Wordsworth

I traveled among unknown men,
In lands beyond the sea;
Nor, England! Did I know till then
What love I bore to thee.

'Tis past, that melancholy dream!
Nor will I quit thy shore
A second time; for still I seem
To love thee more and more.

Among thy mountains did I feel
The joy of my desire;
And she I cherished turned her wheel
Beside an English fire.

Thy mornings showed, thy nights concealed,
The bowers where Lucy played;
And thine too is the last green field
That Lucy's eyes surveyed.

我在陌生人中间旅行

[英]华兹华斯

我在陌生人中间旅行，
到过海外的一个个国度。
啊,英格兰！直到那时我才知道，
我对你的爱是多么深厚。

消逝了,那忧伤的梦！
我再也不会离开你的海岸，
因为我越来越爱你，
爱我的故土家园。

在你的群山中间我感受到
我所期望的欢乐；
我珍爱的她
在英式的炉火旁转动着她的纺车。

露茜玩耍的凉亭
在晨光里显现,在夜幕里隐没；
露茜的眼睛最后掠过的
是你的绿野平畴。

In Memoriam（130）

Alfred Tennyson

Thy voice is on the rolling air;

I here thee where the waters run;

Thou standest in the rising sun,

And in the setting thou art fair.

What art thou then? I cannot guess;

But tho' I seem in star and flower

To feel thee some diffusive power,

I do not therefore love thee less;

怀 念(130)

[英]丁尼生(1809—1892)

你的声音跟随着那翻腾的风,

我听见你的话语融进了潺潺的水声。

你伴着朝阳冉冉升起,

落日的余晖又映出你秀美的仪容。

你现在做什么?我猜不中;

你的活力已经弥漫在星空与花丛,

不管怎样,我对你的爱慕

将与天地一样永恒。

* 此诗与本书第25页的《汹涌吧,大海》皆为诗人怀念挚友和妹夫阿瑟·哈勒木(1811—1833)之作。《怀念》一书写作过程长达17年,此篇编号130。

My love involves the love before;

My love is vaster passion now;

Tho' mix'd with God and Nature thou,

I seem to love thee more and more.

Far off thou art, but ever high;

I have thee still, and I rejoice;

I prosper, circled with thy voice;

I shall not lose thee tho' I die.

我的爱慕包含了前世的爱，

我的爱慕已成为博大的激情。

虽然你跟上帝和自然融为一体，

我的爱慕依然与日俱增。

越升越高，远去了你的身影，

但我们仍旧拥有你，我深感庆幸，

周围萦绕着你的音容，我受益终生，

我不会失去你，即便我葬身丘垄。

Break, Break, Break

Alfred Tennyson

Break, break, break,

On the cold gray stones, O Sea!

And I would that my tongue could utter

The thoughts that arise in me.

O, well for the fisherman's boy,

That he shouts with his sister at play!

O, well for the sailor lad,

That he sings in his boat on the bay!

汹涌吧，大海

[英]丁尼生

汹涌吧，汹涌吧，

啊，大海！你的波涛拍击着冰冷的灰岩；

我多想能够倾吐

心中升腾而起的夙愿。

哦，那渔夫的孩子多么幸运，

兄妹嬉戏，笑语声喧；

哦，那年轻的水手多么幸运，

他在小船上唱歌，小船舶在海湾。

And the stately ships go on

To their haven under the hill;

But O for the touch of a vanished hand,

And the sound of a voice that is still!

Break, break, break,

At the foot of thy crags, O sea!

But the tender grace of a day that is dead

Will never come back to me.

威严的船队在行进,

驶向那山脚下的港湾;

可是,我怎样才能握住那双消失的手,

我怎样才能听到那已经息声的呼喊!

汹涌吧,汹涌吧,

啊,大海！你的波涛还在拍击着悬崖脚下的岩石,

可是,那消失了的温馨和优雅,

再不会回到我的身边。

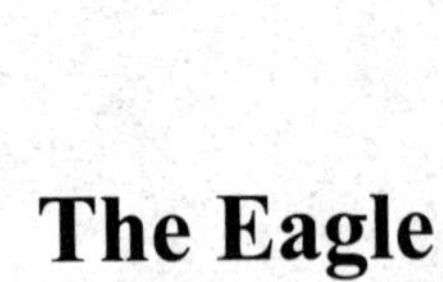

The Eagle

Alfred Tennyson

扫 码 听 诗

He clasps the crag with crooked hands;

Close to the sun in lonely lands,

Ringed with the azure world,he stands.

The wrinkled sea beneath him crawls;

He watches from his mountain walls,

And like a thunderbolt he falls.

鹰

[英]丁尼生

用如钩的爪，抓住悬岩，

在孤寂的国土上，近太阳站着，

周围是天宇的一片蔚蓝。

从岩壁上放眼瞭望，

波涛起伏的海面伸向天边。

突然，它纵身飞下，疾如闪电。

Crossing the Bar

Alfred Tennyson

扫码听诗

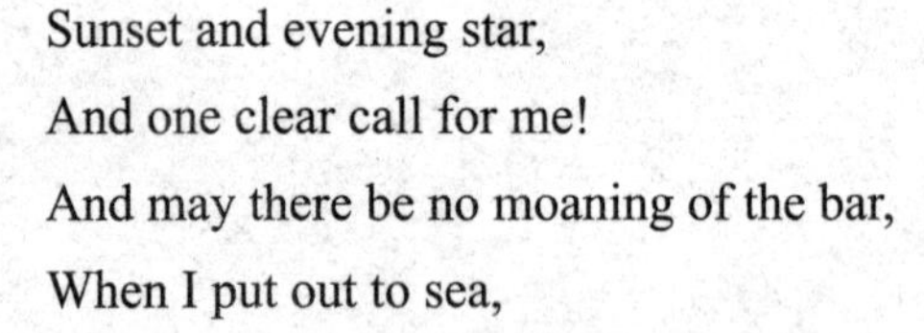

Sunset and evening star,
And one clear call for me!
And may there be no moaning of the bar,
When I put out to sea,

But such a tide as moving seems asleep,
Too full for sound and foam,
When that which drew from out the boundless deep
Turns again home.

Twilight and evening bell,
And after that the dark!
And may there be no sadness of farewell,
When I embark;

For though from out our bourne of Time and Place
The flood may bear me far,
I hope to see my Pilot face to face
When I have crossed the bar.

驶过沙洲[1]

[英]丁尼生

太阳落山,金星闪亮,
一个清晰的声音把我召唤[2]!
但愿这沙洲没有呜咽的涛声,
当我登船离岸。

这汹涌的潮水似乎已经入睡,
涨满了海峡,没有了泡沫和声响,
那些发自海底深处的灵魂,
又一次返回故乡[3]。

黄昏时分,晚钟敲响,
夜幕笼罩了海面!
但愿没有诀别的忧伤,
当我登船离岸。

从时空的边界出发,
虽说这潮水能把我带向远方,
当我驶过沙洲,
我真想面见我的领港④。

① 此诗写于 1889 年,穿越索伦特海峡返回怀特岛的故乡之时,实为诗人告别人世之作。诗人死前数日嘱其家人,此后刊印诗集均以此诗殿后。

② 指死神的召唤。

③ 指个人的灵魂回归自然,与宇宙的灵魂合一。

④ 指上帝。

Meeting at Night

Robert Browning

扫 码 听 诗

The gray sea and the long black land;

And the yellow half-moon large and low;

And the startled little waves that leap

In fiery ringlets from their sleep,

As I gain the cove with pushing prow,

And quench its speed i' the slushy sand.

Then a mile of warm sea-scented beach;

Three fields to cross till a farm appears;

A tap at the pane, the quick sharp scratch

And blue spurt of a lighted match,

And a voice less loud, through its joys and fears,

Than the two hearts beating each to each!

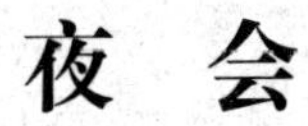

夜 会

[英]罗伯特·布朗宁(1812—1889)

灰蒙蒙的海,黑土地连绵,

黄澄澄半个月亮低悬,

受惊的细浪从睡梦中醒来,

跳动着,一个个似火的金环。

我来到那岬角尖尖的海湾,

慢慢地,慢慢地登上泥浆般的沙滩。

走过温暖的海滩,

海的气味沁人心田,

连绵的田野那边,一座农舍映入眼帘。

轻敲窗,火柴的蓝光一闪,

低语声里透出惊喜与不安,

相见,两颗心跳动着一样的情缘!

Parting at Morning

Robert Browning

Round the cape of a sudden came the sea,

And the sun looked over the mountain's rim:

And straight was a path of gold for him,

And the need of a world of men for me.

晨 别

[英]罗伯特·布朗宁

转过那岬角,大海突然出现在眼前,

太阳升起,端详着山坡的容颜。

海面为它铺了一条金色的路,

真想让芸芸众生来到我身边。

Home Thoughts from Abroad

Robert Browning

1

Oh, to be in England

Now that April's there,

And whoever wakes in England

Sees, some morning, unaware,

That the lowest boughs and the brushwood sheaf

Round the elm-tree bole are in tiny leaf,

While the chaffinch sings on the orchard bough

In England—now!

2

And after April, when May follows,

And the whitethroat builds, and all the swallows!

海外思乡曲

［英］罗伯特·布朗宁

1

哦,在英格兰

正是四月天,

有谁在那里一朝醒来

会意外地发现

那低低的枝条上,那榆树周围的柴捆上,

都长出了细小的叶片,

果园的树枝上传来花鸡的鸣啭,

就现在——在英格兰!

2

四月过后是五月,

燕子翻飞,林莺忙搭窝。

Hark, where my blossomed pear-tree in the hedge

Leans to the field and scatters on the clover

Blossoms and dewdrops—at the bent spray's edge—

That's the wise thrush; he sings each song twice over,

Lest you should think he never could recapture

The first fine careless rapture!

And though the fields look rough with hoary dew,

All will be gay when noontide wakes anew

The buttercups, the little children's dower

—Far brighter than this gaudy melon-flower!

听,柴篱内开花的梨树

把枝丫伸向田野,在苜蓿丛上

撒下梨花片片如雪似雾,还有弯弯枝条上的露珠——

听,那是聪明的鸫,每首歌至少要唱两遍,

要不然,你会以为它不知重温

那轻松而美好的初欢。

田野里白露如霜,看来有些蓬乱,

一旦正午苏醒了毛茛,一切将变得生意盎然。

毛茛是孩子们的彩礼,

——远比这边*俗艳的葫芦花美丽。

* 指意大利——译者注。

Comfort's in Heaven

William Shakespeare

扫 码 听 诗

Comfort's in heaven;

and we are on the earth,

Where nothing lives but crosses,

cares and grief.

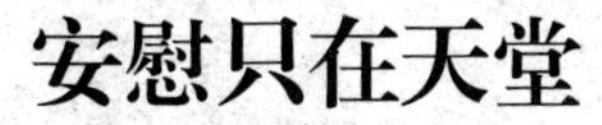

安慰只在天堂

［英］莎士比亚（1564—1616）

安慰只在天堂，

我们活在地上。

地上何所有？

愁苦与忧伤。

I Pray You

William Shakespeare

Yet, I pray you:

But with the word

the time will bring on summer,

When briers shall have leaves as well as thorns,

And be as sweet as sharp.

我求你，且等待

［英］莎士比亚

我求你，且等待，

夏天就要到来。

野蔷薇虽然遍身棘刺，

却也有葳蕤绿叶覆盖。

纵然是锋芒尖厉，

却也是芬芳可爱。

Work without Hope

Samuel Taylor Coleridge

All Nature seems at works. Slugs leave their lair—

The bees are stirring—birds are on the wing—

And winter slumbering in the open air,

Wears on his smiling face a dream of Spring!

And I the while, the sole unbusy thing,

Nor honey make, nor pair, nor build, nor sing.

Yet well I ken the banks where amaranths blow,

Have traced the fount whence streams of nectar flow.

Bloom O ye amaranths! Bloom for whom ye may,

For me ye bloom not! Glide, rich streams, away!

With lips unbrightened, wreathless brow, I stroll:

And would learn the spells that drowse my soul?

Work without Hope draws nectar in a sieve,

And Hope without an object cannot live.

没有希望的工作

［英］柯勒律治（1772—1834）

整个自然界都在忙忙碌碌，

蚰蜒出洞穴，蜜蜂闹嘤嘤，鸟儿飞向天空——

寒冬在露天昏睡，

微笑的脸庞上映出春天的梦！

我此刻是唯一的闲人，

不酿蜜，不营造，不唱歌，也不结伴行。

然而我熟知，不凋花*绽放的那些河岸，

我追寻泉源，找到那流淌着花蜜的溪流。

绽放吧，不凋花！愿意为谁就为谁

只不要为我绽放！流走吧，那花蜜的溪流！

我东游西转，带着晦暗的嘴唇，没有花冠的额头；

能不能学会让我的灵魂昏睡的魔咒？

没有希望的工作，就是让花蜜筛上流，

没有目标的希望，不可能长久。

* 不凋花：想象中的一种花。

To the Virgin: To Make Much of Time

Robert Herrick

Gather ye rose-buds while ye may,
Old time is still a-flying:
And this same flower that smiles today,
Tomorrow will be dying.

The glorious lamp of heaven, the Sun,
The higher he's a-getting
The sooner will his race be run,
And nearer he's to setting.

That age is the best which is the first,
When youth and blood are warmer;
But being spent, the worse, and worst
Times still succeed the former.

Then be not coy, but use your time,
And while ye may, go marry;
For having lost but once your prime,
You may for ever tarry.

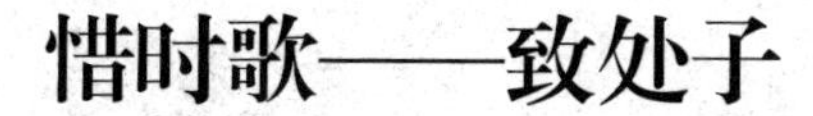

惜时歌——致处子

［英］罗伯特·赫里克（1591—1674）

趁年轻，把玫瑰花蕾采集，
地老天荒，时光穿行如飞。
看今朝鲜花吐艳，
到明天叶落花残。

太阳是寰宇的神灯，
它越升越高，到达中天，
它匆匆赶路，追风逐电，
越高越快越近西山。

最可贵是少年时，
生气勃勃，血气温煦。
可惜岁月磨蚀，
桑榆暮景终可期。

珍惜你的青春，
及时出嫁行大礼。
韶华一旦失，
终生延误经不起。

Little Gidding

Thomas Stearns Eliot

The dove descending breaks the air

With flame of incandescent terror

Of which the tongues declare

The one discharge from sin and error.

The one hope, or else despair

Lies in the choice of pyre or pyre—

To be redeemed from fire by fire.

Who then devised the torment? Love.

Love is the unfamiliar Name

Behind the hands that wove

The intolerable shirt of flame

Which human power cannot remove.

We only live, only suspire

Consumed by either fire or fire.

小小的吉丁村

[英]艾略特(1888—1965)

鸽子飞下,划破了天空,

带着光彩夺目的恐怖的火焰;

众口一词,都说

这火消除了谬误,解脱了孽缘。

唯一的希望,也许是绝望,

就在于选择火葬的柴堆,

在熊熊烈火中把孽债清偿。

谁设计了此等酷刑? 爱神。

对那些魔爪,爱情是个陌生的名称。

他们会编织不堪忍受的火焰的套衫,

人的力量无法脱出。

我们只有活着,我们只有长叹,

渐渐地被火吞噬,在火中消散。

A Birthday

Christina Georgina Rossetti

My heart is like a singing bird
Whose nest is in a watered shoot;
My heart is like an apple tree
Whose boughs are bent with thickset fruit;
My heart is like a rainbow shell
That paddles in a halcyon sea;
My heart is gladder than all these
Because my love is come to me.

Raise me a dais of silk and down;
Hang it with vair and purple dyes;
Carve it in doves, and pomegranates,
And peacocks with a hundred eyes;
Work it in gold and silver grapes,
In leaves and silver fleurs-de-lys;
Because the birthday of my life
Is come, my love is come to me.

生 日

[英]罗塞蒂(1830—1894)

我的心像一只正在唱歌的鸟,
湿漉漉的新枝上有它的爱巢,
我的心像一棵苹果树,
果实累累压弯了枝条。
我的心像一只七彩的贝壳,
在平静的海里轻轻飘摇。
我的心比它们都快活,
我亲爱的人就要来到。

给我搭建一座高台,配上丝绸和绒羽的华彩,
饰以绛紫的色调,和相隔相间的青白;
刻上鸽子的安详,石榴的红火,
还有那百个翎斑的孔雀,
绣上一串串的金银葡萄,
青枝绿叶掩映着美丽的纹章——百合;
因为我的生日来临,
我亲爱的人要来见我。

Remember

Christina Georgina Rossetti

扫 码 听 诗

Remember me when I am gone away,

Gone far away in to the silent land;

When you can no more hold me by the hand,

Nor I half turn to go yet turning stay.

Remember me when no more day by day

You tell me of our future that you planned:

Only remember me; you understand

It will be late to counsel then or pray.

Yet if you should forget me for a while

And afterwards remember, do not grieve:

For if the darkness and corruption leave

A vestige of the thoughts that once I had,

Better by far you should forget and smile

Than that you should remember and be sad.

记　住

[英]罗塞蒂

记住我，当我从这儿走开，

走向那远方的无声世界，

你再也不能和我牵手，

命运也不容我犹疑徘徊。

记住我，当你不再能和我娓娓谈，

日复一日，筹划我们的明天，

只是要把我记在心间，

你知道，商量和祈祷都为时已晚。

要是你曾把我遗忘，

后来想起，不要悲伤，

虽说是黑暗与腐朽不留情面，

我思想的痕迹还是会留下一点；

因此你应该忘却，应该笑，

远胜过刻骨铭心，空自忧伤。

The Echoing Green

William Blake

The sun does arise,

And make happy the skies;

The merry bells ring

To welcome the spring;

The skylark and the thrush,

The birds of the bush,

Sing louder around

To the bell's cheerful sound;

While our sport shall be seen

On the Echoing Green.

回声缭绕的绿草地

[英]威廉·布莱克(1757—1827)

太阳升起来，

天空乐开怀。

欢乐钟声响，

迎接春姑娘。

云雀画眉不等闲，

林鸟争鸣,与钟声汇成欢乐的交响，

健身的人们涌现在

回声缭绕的绿草地上。

The Sick Rose

William Blake

O rose, thou art sick.

The invisible worm

That flies in the night

In the howling storm

Has found out thy bed

Of crimson joy,

And his dark secret love

Does thy life destroy.

病玫瑰

[英]威廉·布莱克

啊,玫瑰,你病得不轻

你可知有种无形的小虫,

常在黑夜里出没,

在呼啸的风暴中飞行。

它发现了你的花坛,

那一片欢乐的绯红。

它隐秘幽暗的爱,

将毁掉你的一生。

The Clod and the Pebble

William Blake

"Love seeketh not Itself to please,

Nor for itself hath any care;

But for another gives its ease,

And builds a Heaven in Hell's despair."

So sang a little Clod of Clay,

Trodden with the cattle's feet;

But a Pebble of the brook,

Warbled out these meters meet:

"Love seeketh only Self to please,

To bind another to its delight,

Joys in another's loss of ease,

And builds a Hell in Heaven's despite."

土块与卵石

[英]威廉·布莱克

“爱情不为自己乐，

只把安宁舒适给予另一个。

奋不顾身,为的是

在地狱的绝望中造一个天堂。”

一个土块这样唱，

牛羊踩踏全不放心上。

清清溪水一卵石，

唱的歌儿不一样：

“爱情只为自己乐，

把别人捆在一起寻快活，

让别人失去安宁和舒适，

损毁了天堂,造个地狱把日子过。”

The Chimney Sweeper

William Blake

A little black thing among the snow,

Crying, " 'weep! 'weep!" in notes of woe!

"Where are thy father and mother? Say?"

"They are both gone up to the church to pray."

"Because I was happy upon the heath,

And smiled among the winter's snow,

They clothed me in the clothes of death,

And taught me to sing the notes of woe."

"And because I am happy and dance and sing,

They think they have done me no injury,

And are gone to praise God and his priest and king,

Who make up a heaven of our misery."

扫烟囱的孩子

[英]威廉·布莱克

一个小孩,一身黑衣,出现在雪地上。

他在喊叫:“哭!哭吧!”声音凄凉。

“你的父母在哪里?讲?”

“为祈祷,他们去了教堂。”

“因为我在这荒原觉得很好,

在冬天的雪地露出微笑,

他们给我穿上丧服,

教我唱歌,用悲哀的声调。”

“看我唱歌又跳舞,他们以为

没给我带来什么损伤和痛苦,

他们去赞美上帝,还有神父和国王,

用我们的苦难造就了天堂。”

Leisure

William Henry Davies

扫码听诗

What is this life if, full of care,
We have no time to stand and stare?

No time to stand beneath the boughs,
And stare as long as sheep and cows;

No time to see the woods we pass,
Where squirrels hide their nuts in grass;

No time to see, in broad daylight,
Streams full of stars, like skies at night;

No time to turn at Beauty's glance,
And watch her feet, how they can dance.

A poor life this if, full of care,
We have no time to stand and stare.

悠 闲

[英]威廉·亨利·戴维斯(1871—1940)

这算什么生活,倘若焦虑不安,
没时间驻足赏玩?

没时间站在树枝下,
像牛羊那样久久地凝目望远。

没有时间看一看我们经过的树林,
那里松鼠正把榛果藏在草间。

没时间在日光下,
看溪流里星虫星散,像那繁星满天。

没时间回头迎接那美神的一瞥,
看看她双脚怎样舞翩翩。

这生活实在可怜,如果你焦虑不安,
没时间驻足赏玩。

The Villain

William Henry Davies

扫 码 听 诗

While joy gave clouds the light of stars,

That beamed where'er they looked;

And calves and lambs had tottering knees,

Excited, while they sucked;

While every bird enjoyed his song,

Without one thought of harm or wrong—

I turned my head and saw the wind,

Not far from where I stood,

Dragging the corn by her golden hair,

Into a dark and lonely wood.

无 赖

[英]威廉·亨利·戴维斯

繁星点点照亮了云彩，

把星光投射到四方八面。

牛犊和羊羔脚步蹒跚，

兴致勃勃吃奶欢。

小鸟个个都欣赏自己的歌儿好，

全不顾破了啥规范——

蓦然回首，见风儿

就在那边，离我不远。

他抓住玉米的金发，

把她拖进幽暗的荒林里面。

第二辑

风狂雨骤的夜晚

The Silken Tent

Robert Frost

扫 码 听 诗

She is as in a field a silken tent

At midday when the sunny summer breeze

Has dried the dew and all its ropes relent,

So that in guys it gently sways at ease,

And its supporting central cedar pole,

That is its pinnacle to heavenward

And signifies the sureness of the soul,

Seems to owe naught to any single cord,

But strictly held by none, is loosely bound

By countless silken ties of love and thought

To everything on earth the compass round,

And only by one's going slightly taut

In the capriciousness of summer air

Is of the slightest bondage made aware.

丝织的帐篷

[美]弗罗斯特(1874—1963)

她像是田野里的一顶丝织的帐篷,

阳光灿灿的夏日,露水

在正午的微风中消融,

丝帐轻摇,摇出一片安闲与宁静。

它的中央是一根雪松做的支柱,

高高的尖顶指向蔚蓝的天空,

象征着灵魂的坚定、爱的坚贞。

那支柱似乎不靠任何单独的牵索,

它靠的是无数用爱和理念编织的丝绳,

松缓地联结到地球上的物事万种。

只有当刮起变幻莫测的夏风,

丝帐才显得绷紧,

让人意识到它在轻微的约束之中。

Acquainted with the Night

Robert Frost

扫 码 听 诗

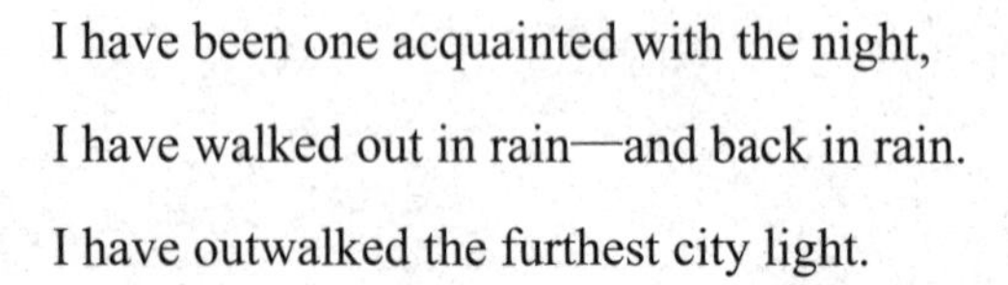
I have been one acquainted with the night,
I have walked out in rain—and back in rain.
I have outwalked the furthest city light.

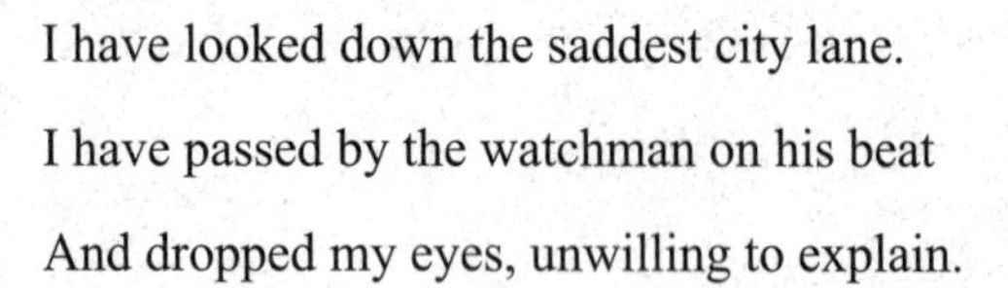
I have looked down the saddest city lane.
I have passed by the watchman on his beat
And dropped my eyes, unwilling to explain.

I have stood still and stopped the sound of feet
When far away an interrupted cry
Came over houses from another street,
But not to call me back or say good-bye;
And further still at an unearthly height,
One luminary clock against the sky

Proclaimed the time was neither wrong nor right.
I have been one acquainted with the night.

我做了夜的朋友

[美]弗罗斯特

我做了夜的朋友，
冒雨出行，把城郊的万家灯火抛在身后，
归途上，风未消歇雨未收。

我徘徊在悲凉的小巷，
从巡夜人的身边，
无言走过，垂下目光。

我停下脚步，静静地站住，
远处传来一声叫喊，
从另一条街，越过屋舍墙垣。
不是叫我回家，不是与我再见。
再往前，一只发光的钟，
衬着那幽黑的夜空高悬。

它宣告：这时间无功也无咎。
我做了夜的朋友。

Never Again Would Bird's Song Be the Same

Robert Frost

He would declare and could himself believe

That the birds there in all the garden round

From having heard the daylong voice of Eve

Had added to their own an oversound,

Her tone of meaning but without the words.

Admittedly an eloquence so soft

Could only have had an influence on birds

When call or laughter carried it aloft.

Be that as may be, she was in their song.

Moreover her voice upon their voices crossed

Had now persisted in the woods so long

That probably it never would be lost.

Never again would bird's song be the same.

And to do that to birds was why she came.

鸟儿的歌声再也不像以前

[美]弗罗斯特

那一次,夏娃的呼叫响了一整天,

声音传遍了周围的所有林园。

这无词的声响隐含着深意,

鸟儿的鸣声从此受到感染。

——他相信是这样,他这样断言。[①]

说实话,受影响的也只有鸟儿的鸣叫,

因为那声音轻柔和婉,

夹着笑声和呼唤传到林间。

就这样,她活在它们的歌声里,

她的喊叫和百鸟的齐鸣打成一片。

这声音一直在林子里回荡,

也许就永不消散。

鸟儿的歌声从此再也不像往常,

正是为鸟儿做这点事,她才来到人间。

①他,指亚当。

Desert Places

Robert Frost

Snow falling and night falling fast, oh, fast
In a field I looked into going past,
And the ground almost covered smooth in snow,
But a few weeds and stubble showing last.

The woods around it have it—it is theirs.
All animals are smothered in their lairs.
I am too absent-spirited to count:
The loneliness includes me unawares.

As lonely as it is, that loneliness
Will be more lonely ere it will be less—
A blanker whiteness of benighted snow
With no expression, nothing to express.

They cannot scare me with their empty spaces
Between stars—on stars where no human race is.
I have it in me so much nearer home
To scare myself with my own desert places.

荒　漠

［美］弗罗斯特

夜幕下，雪花纷纷，
在田野我追寻渐渐逝去的光阴。
大地蒙上了雪的厚被，
剩几棵野草残株，一片萧森。

动物们全都憋进了洞穴，
拥抱这雪野的，只有周边的树林。
可怜我漫不经心，不知不觉，
竟然也陷进这死寂荒漠的围困。

寂寞笼罩一切，万籁无声，
这寂寞还会增长，落得个
白茫茫的大地真干净。
那白雪无言无语，没有表情。

我不怕星际的洪荒，
那星球上渺无人烟。
倒是离家越近，
我自身的一片片荒漠让我心寒。

The Oven Bird

Robert Frost

There is a singer everyone has heard,

Loud, a mid-summer and a mid-wood bird,

Who makes the solid tree trunks sound again.

He says that leaves are old and that for flowers

Mid-summer is to spring as one to ten.

He says the early petal-fall is past

When pear and cherry bloom went down in showers

On sunny days a moment overcast;

And comes that other fall we name the fall.

He says the highway dust is over all.

The bird would cease and be as other birds

But that he knows in singing not to sing.

The question that he frames in all but words

Is what to make of a diminished thing.

灶　鸟

［美］弗罗斯特

他是仲夏时节的林鸟，

作为歌手，那是大名鼎鼎，

嗓门大，他一叫枝摇树有声。

他唱道：树叶老，百花残，

春天的繁华褪去了大半。

等到那晴朗日子的忧愁时刻，

樱花与梨花纷纷飘落，

金色的早秋也将退尽灿烂，

迎来的是一个寂寥的秋天。

公路上尘土飞扬，

这鸟儿不再鸣叫，像别的鸟一样。

不过他知道该唱就唱，该息声时就息声。

到最后他归结出来一个疑问：

怎样去理解那渐渐衰落的物事人情？

Fire and Ice

Robert Frost

扫 码 听 诗

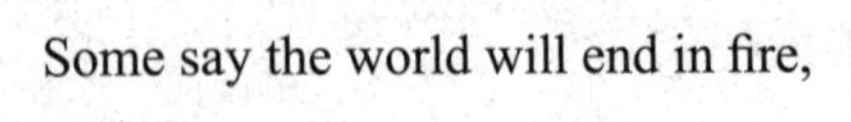

Some say the world will end in fire,

Some say in ice.

From what I've tasted of desire

I hold with those who favor fire.

But if it had to perish twice,

I think I know enough of hate

To say that for destruction ice

Is also great

And would suffice.

火与冰

[美]弗罗斯特

世界将毁于火海,还是冰川?

人们有不同的意见。

依照我的趣向,

我站在火海说的一边。

不过,要是它须毁灭两次,

我也有足够的愤恨断言:

让冰川把这世界变成汪洋一片。

Wild Night—Wild Nights!

Emily Dickinson

Wild Nights—Wild Nights!

Were I with thee

Wild Nights should be

Our luxury!

Futile—the winds—

To a Heart in port—

Done with the Compass—

Done with the Chart!

Rowing in Eden

Ah, the Sea!

Might I but moor—Tonight—

In Thee!

风狂雨骤，这狂野的夜晚！

[美]狄金森（1830—1886）

风狂雨骤，这狂野的夜晚，

要是有你在身旁，

狂野的夜晚，

就该是我们的盛宴！

无用的——任凭你风雨如磐，

一颗心已经有了停泊的港湾。

不要那海图，

不要那罗盘！

一往直前，划行在伊甸园！

啊，大海！

我情愿——今夜——

在你的风涛里泊舟靠岸。

There Is No Frigate Like a Book

Emily Dickinson

There is no frigate like a book

To take us lands away,

Nor any coursers like a page

Of prancing poetry.

This traverse may the poorest take

Without oppress of toll;

How frugal is the chariot

That bears a human soul!

书籍胜过舰船

[美]狄金森

越洋过海，轻舟巨舰，

比不上书籍的威力无边。

快马加鞭，日行千里，

比不上神思飞扬的诗篇。

思想的摆渡不会撂下穷苦人，

不会强收一个铜板。

载运人类灵魂的轻车，

竟是这样地朴素简单。

Because I Could Not Stop for Death

Emily Dickinson

Because I could not stop for Death,

He kindly stopped for me—

The carriage held but just ourselves

And Immortality.

We slowly drove—he knew no haste,

And I had put away

My labor and my leisure too,

For His Civility.

We passed the school, where children strove,

At recess, in the ring,

We passed the fields of gazing grain,

We passed the setting sun,

我不能停下等死神

[美]狄金森

我不能停下等死神，

他恂恂有礼，驾车接鄙人——

车上的乘客就两个，

还有永恒也在座。

马车慢慢行——急急忙忙他可用不着，

我也放下了我的工作，

还有我的娱乐，

为报答他的恭谨与谦和。

我们经过学校，孩子们下了课，

围成一圈正斗乐；

我们穿越田野，庄稼瞧着马车过；

我们经过夕阳，看着它慢慢朝西落。

Or rather, he passed us;

The dews drew quivering and chill—

For only gossamer, my gown;

My tippet, only tulle.

We passed before a house that seemed

A swelling of the ground;

The roof was scarcely visible.

The cornice, In the ground.

Since then, 'tis Centuries, and yet

Feels shorter than the Day

I first surmised the horses' heads

Were toward Eternity.

不,或许应该说夕阳从我们身边过,

露水冰凉,天寒人哆嗦——

我的长袍像轻纱,

披肩像丝网一样薄。

我们停在一座房子前,

那房子就像地上隆起的土包,

屋顶几乎看不见,

窗楣——也埋在土里面。

从那以后——似乎过了几百年,

但感觉比那一天还要短;

那一天马头朝向永恒——

这是我平生头一次做出的推断。

The Lightning Is a Yellow Fork

Emily Dickinson

扫 码 听 诗

The Lightning is a yellow Fork

From Tables in the sky

By inadvertent fingers dropt

The awful Cutlery

Of mansions never quite disclosed

And never quite concealed

The Apparatus of the Dark

To ignorance revealed.

闪电是金黄的叉

［美］狄金森

闪电是金黄的叉，

通过漫不经心的手指

从天宫的餐桌上掉下。

这宫室的刀具令人惊羡，

虽说从未悉数展出，

可也不曾遮遮掩掩。

它们是黑天宇的装备，

向洪荒闪现。

If I Can Stop One Heart from Breaking

Emily Dickinson

If I can stop one heart from breaking,

I shall not live in vain;

If I can ease one life the aching,

Or cool one pain,

Or help one fainting robin

Unto his nest again,

I shall not live in vain.

不让一颗心破碎

［美］狄金森

若能救助一个人，

不让一颗心破碎，

我就不算白活。

若能减轻一个生命的痛苦，

或者帮一只虚弱的鸫鸟回窝，

我就不算白活。

Much Madness Is Divinest Sense

Emily Dickinson

扫码听诗

Much Madness is the divinest Sense—

To a discerning Eye—

Much Sense—the starkest Madness—

'Tis the Majority

In this, as All, prevail—

Assent—and you are sane—

Demur—you're straightaway dangerous—

And handled with a Chain—

疯疯癫癫实乃聪明非凡

[美]狄金森

疯疯癫癫实乃聪明非凡，

有此见识，出自慧眼，

明慧达人倒是十足的疯癫。

多数人的思想

就这样流传——

你同意——算是明智。

你反对——实在危险，

讨一身锁链。

Tell All the Truth But Tell It Slant—

Emily Dickinson

扫 码 听 诗

Tell all the Truth but tell it slant—

Success in Circuit lies

Too bright for our infirm Delight

The Truth's superb surprise

As Lightning to the Children eased

With explanation kind

The Truth must dazzle gradually

Or every man be blind.

真　理

[美]狄金森

要揭示真理的全貌，

但要从侧面讲，听起来有点偏斜——

弯路才是成功的家。

真理的强光，我们脆弱的欣喜受不了它。

真理是最大的惊诧

像儿童看到闪电，

得到亲切的解答。

真理必须渐明渐悟，渐放光华，

要不然就会人人眼瞎。

The Tide Rises, the Tide Falls

Henry Wadsworth Longfellow

扫 码 听 诗

The tide rises, the tide falls,
The twilight darkens, the curlew calls;
Along the sea-sands damp and brown
The traveller hastens toward the town,
　　And the tide rises, the tide falls.

Darkness settles on roofs and walls,
But the sea, the sea in the darkness calls;
The little waves, with their soft, white hands,
Efface the footprints in the sands,
　　And the tide rises, the tide falls.

The morning breaks; the steeds in their stalls
Stamp and neigh, as the hostler calls;
The day returns, but nevermore
Returns the traveller to the shore,
　　And the tide rises, the tide falls.

潮涨，潮落

［美］朗费罗（1807—1882）

潮涨，潮落。
暮色苍茫，鹬鸟在唱歌；
沿着潮湿的褐色沙滩，
旅人匆匆，走向那城郭。
　　潮涨，潮落。

夜色落脚在屋顶和墙垣，
大海在黑暗中呼喊；
轻波碎浪，用柔和的手，
抹去了脚印，抚平了沙滩。
　　潮涨，潮落。

天色破晓，骏马嘶鸣又跺脚，
马夫在呼叫，
开启了新的一天，
旅人再也没有回到海岸。
　　潮涨，潮落。

It Is Not Always May

Henry Wadsworth Longfellow

The sun is bright—the air is clear,

The darting swallows soar and sing.

And from the stately elms I hear,

The bluebird prophesying Spring.

So blue you winding river flows,

It seems an outlet from the sky,

Where waiting till the west-wind blows,

The freighted clouds at anchor lie.

All things are new —the buds, the leaves,

That gild the elm-tree's nodding crest;

And even the nest beneath the eaves;

There are no birds in last year's nest!

不能总是 5 月天

[美]朗费罗

阳光灿烂,空气清新,

翻飞的燕子唱着歌儿冲向云端,

从威严的榆树上,我听见

蓝鸟在预报春天。

曲曲弯弯的河里春水绿如蓝,

像是从天上灌下的清泉,

那里有积雨的云彩待命,

专等着西风起,把甘霖洒向人间。

一切物事都那么新鲜——嫩芽、叶片,

装饰着老榆东摇西摆的树冠,

屋檐下的巢里,

去年的鸟儿再也看不见!

All things rejoice in youth and love,

The fullness of their first delight!

And learn from the soft heavens above

The melting tenderness of night.

Maiden, that read'st this simple rhyme,

Enjoy thy youth, it will not stay;

Enjoy the fragrance of thy prime,

For oh, it is not always May!

Enjoy the Spring of Love and Youth,

To some good angel leave the rest;

For Time will teach thee soon the truth,

There are no birds in last year's nest!

万类尽享青春与爱的愉悦，

最初的欢乐是多么圆满！

那仁慈的上苍，

让你把春夜的似水柔情体验。

你读过这简朴的诗篇，姑娘，

要珍惜你的韶华，它不会停留不前；

要享受你青春的芬芳，

因为：不能总是 5 月天。

把别的事留给善良的天使吧，

尽情地享受你的爱，你的华年！

时光会很快教给你一个真理：

去年的巢里，鸟儿再也看不见。

The Rainy Day

Henry Wadsworth Longfellow

The day is cold, and dark, and dreary
It rains, and the wind is never weary;
The vine still clings to the mouldering wall,
But at every gust the dead leaves fall,
And the day is dark and dreary.

My life is cold, and dark, and dreary;
It rains, and the wind is never weary;
My thoughts still cling to the mouldering Past,
But the hopes of youth fall thick in the blast,
And the days are dark and dreary.

Be still, sad heart! and cease repining;
Behind the clouds is the sun still shining;
Thy fate is the common fate of all,
Into each life some rain must fall,
Some days must be dark and dreary.

雨　天

[美]朗费罗

严寒，昏黑，日子乏味，
雨潇潇，风不息。
葡萄藤依然攀附在残垣断壁，
阵风忽起，枯叶纷纷落满地。
天黑地昏，日子郁闷。

我的生活凄冷，昏暗，枯燥乏味，
雨潇潇，风不息。
我的思绪依然攀附在破落的过去，
但青春的希望却在暴风中崛起。
天黑地昏，日子郁闷。

悲伤的心儿啊，且安静，莫牢骚，
云层后太阳还在照耀。
你的命运就是大众的命运：
每人的生活里都有风雨如磐，
有些日子定会有枯燥与昏暗。

Annabel Lee

Edgar Allan Poe

扫 码 听 诗

It was many and many a year ago,

In a kingdom by the sea,

That a maiden there lived whom you may know

By the name of Annabel Lee;

And this maiden she lived with no other thought

Than to love and be loved by me.

I was a child and she was a child,

In this kingdom by the sea;

But we loved with a love that was more than love—

I and my Annabel Lee;

With a love that the winged seraphs of heaven

Coveted her and me.

安纳波·李*

[美]埃德加·爱伦·坡(1809—1849)

这故事发生在很多很多年以前,

有一个王国坐落在海边。

那里住着一个姑娘,

安纳波·李的芳名天下传。

除了爱我又被我爱,

她没有别的心愿。

那时候我们都是孩子,

生活在这个国度,在海边。

我们的爱非比寻常,

就连天使也垂涎。

* 此诗系作者悼念去世时年仅27岁的妻子弗吉尼亚·克莱姆之作。

And this was the reason that, long ago,

In this kingdom by the sea,

A wind blew out of a cloud, chilling

My beautiful Annabel Lee;

So that her high-born kinsmen came

And bore her away from me,

To shut her up in a sepulchre

In this kingdom by the sea.

The angels, not half so happy in heaven,

Went envying her and me—

Yes! that was the reason (as all men know,

In this kingdom by the sea)

That the wind came out of the cloud by night,

Chilling and killing my Annabel Lee.

多年前，多年前的一个夜晚，

狂风大作乌云翻。

安纳波冻得发抖，

她的亲属把她带走，从我的身边。

他们把她关进一个墓穴，

就在这个王国，在海边。

在天堂，天使们并不快乐，

见我俩相亲相爱，他们妒火中烧，

因此才有了那次乌云翻滚狂风大作，

冻死了我的安纳波。

But our love it was stronger by far than the love

Of those who were older than we—

Of many far wiser than we—

And neither the angels in heaven above,

Nor the demons down under the sea,

Can ever dissever my soul from the soul

Of the beautiful Annabel Lee;

For the moon never beams without bringing me dreams

Of the beautiful Annabel Lee;

And the stars never rise but I feel the bright eyes

Of the beautiful Annabel Lee;

And so, all the night-tide, I lie down by the side

Of my darling—my darling—my life and my bride,

In the sepulchre there by the sea—

In her tomb by the sounding sea.

比起那些年长的人，

比起那些明智者，

我们的爱情远远超过。

不管是天上的天使，

不管是海底下的恶魔，

谁也不能把我们的灵魂分割。

月光溶溶，光波中总有安纳波的旧梦，

繁星点点，星光中总是闪动着安纳波晶莹的眼睛。

晚潮中，我整夜躺在海边，

身旁是我的最亲，我的新娘，我的生命，

就在她的墓穴里，

耳边传来大海的隆隆涛声。

The Long Voyage

Malcolm Cowley

Not that the pines were darker there,
Nor mid-May dogwood brighter there,
Nor swifts more swift in summer air;
It was my own country,

Having its thunderclap of spring,
Its long midsummer ripening,
Its corn hoar-stiff at harvesting,
Almost like any country,

Yet being mine; its face, its speech,
Its hills bent low within my reach,
Its river birch and upland beech
Were mine, of my own country.

Now the dark waters at the bow
Fold back, like earth against the plow;
Foam brightens like the dogwood now
At home, in my own country.

远　航

［美］马尔科姆·考利（1898—1989）

不是那里的松树更幽暗，
不是那里5月的红柳更明丽，
不是夏日的雨燕轻捷地飞，
那是我们的祖国，装在心里。

阳春惊蛰，听雷声隆隆，
仲夏绵长，有物事成熟的情趣。
收获季，玉米棒子长着白须，
风景不殊，每个国度都如此。

就因为那个国家是我的，她的面貌和言语亲切无比，
她的一座座逶迤的山丘，我上得去，
她河畔的白桦、高地的山毛榉，
都是我的，都是祖国的拱壁。

眼前这幽暗的海水在船头回旋，
就像那犁铧前翻滚的黑泥，
泡沫闪亮，像那家乡的红柳，
长在祖国自己的大地。

I Saw in Louisiana a Live-Oak Growing

Walt Whitman

I saw in Louisiana a live-oak growing,
All alone stood it and the moss hung down from the
    branches,
Without any companion it grew there uttering joyous
    leaves of dark green,
And its look, rude, unbending, lusty, made me think of myself;
But I wonder'd how it could utter joyous leaves standing
    alone there without its friend near, for I knew I could not,
And I broke off a twig with a certain number of leaves
    upon it, and twined around it a little moss,
And brought it away, and I have placed it in sight in my room,
It is not needed to remind me as of my own dear friends,
(For I believe lately I think of little else than of them,)
Yet it remains to me a curious token, it makes me think
    of manly love;
For all that, and though the live-oak glistens there in
    Louisiana solitary in a wide flat space,
Uttering joyous leaves all its life without a friend a lover near,
I know very well I could not.

在路易斯安那，我看见一棵活力迸发的橡树在成长

[美]惠特曼(1819—1892)

在路易斯安那，我看见一棵活力迸发的橡树在成长，
它孤单单地挺立在大地上，细细的苔丝从枝条上垂下，
它没有伴侣，深绿的叶子摇曳出一片欢乐的喧哗。
它的粗犷、挺拔，还有勃勃的生机，都让我想起我自家。
我不懂，它怎能挺立在那儿，没有朋友的陪伴，竟能
　　长出欢乐的叶子，我知道我不行，像它那样的活法。
我折下一根有苔丝缠绕的带叶的枝条，
把它放在我的屋里，好随时看见它，
我没有必要借助它使我想起亲爱的朋友，
(我相信最近经常想起他们，)
不过它仍然是一个奇异的象征，它让我想起高尚的爱情；
尽管如此，这活力迸发的橡树孤单单地闪耀在
　　路易斯安那的原野，
没有朋友，没有情人，却长出那么多欢乐的叶子，
我知道我不行，像它那样的活法。

The Negro Speaks of Rivers

Langston Hughes

I’ve known rivers:
I’ve known rivers ancient as the world and older than the flow of human blood in human rivers.

My soul has grown deep like the rivers.

I bathed in the Euphrates when dawns were young
I built my hut near the Congo and it lulled me to sleep.
I looked upon the Nile and raised the pyramids above it.
I heard the singing of the Mississippi when Abe Lincoln went down to New Orleans, and I've seen its muddy bosom turn all golden in the sunset

I’ve known rivers:
Ancient, dusky rivers.

My soul has grown deep like the rivers.

听黑人讲河的故事

[美]兰斯顿·休斯(1902—1967)

我结识了许多河川，
和这个世界一起,它们经历了地老天荒，
当它们横空出世，
鲜红的血液尚未在人的体内流淌。

我的灵魂变得深邃,像大河一样。

我曾在幼发拉底河沐浴，
当大地初露霞光。
我在刚果河畔盖了棚屋一座，
水声潺湲,哄诱我进入梦乡。
我朝尼罗河张望,让一座座金字塔耸立在河域的上方。
我听见密西西比河在唱歌,那时节
亚伯·林肯正走向新奥尔良。我看见
他沾满泥土的前胸,阳光下发出灿灿金光。

我结识了许多河川，
古老的、忧郁的长河大江。

我的灵魂变得深邃,像大河一样。

Words Like Freedom

扫码听诗

Langston Hughes

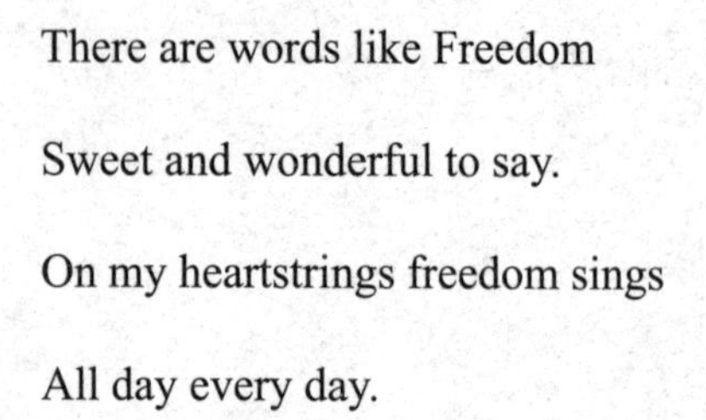

There are words like Freedom

Sweet and wonderful to say.

On my heartstrings freedom sings

All day every day.

There are words like Liberty

That almost make me cry.

If you had known what I know

You would know why.

像自由这种字眼

[美]兰斯顿·休斯

像自由这种字眼，

说起来漂亮，听起来舒畅，

每时每刻

它在我的心弦上振荡。

像解放这种字眼

我一听几乎要哭，

要是你知道我所知的一切，

你就会明白其中的缘故。

Warning

Langston Hughes

扫 码 听 诗

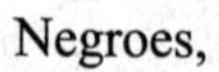

Negroes,

Sweet and docile,

Meek, humble and kind:

Beware the day

They change their mind!

Wind

In the cotton fields,

Gentle Breeze:

Beware the hour

It uproots trees!

警　告

[美]兰斯顿·休斯

黑人，

和蔼可亲，

谦和，善良，温顺。

当心有一天，

他们会改变主意。

风

在棉田里游荡，

暖煦和畅，

当心有个时刻

它会把大树拔起。

Dreams

Langston Hughes

Hold fast to dreams

For if dreams die

Life is a broken-winged bird

That cannot fly.

Hold fast to dreams

For when dreams go

Life is a barren field

Frozen with snow.

梦　想

[美]兰斯顿·休斯

坚守你的梦想。

倘若梦想破灭，

生活就是断了翅膀的鸟，

再也不能飞翔。

坚守你的梦想。

倘若梦想消失，

生活就是冰封雪冻的荒野，

芜秽而凄凉。

Domination of Black

Wallace Stevens

At night, by the fire,
The colors of the bushes
And of the fallen leaves,
Repeating themselves,
Turned in the room,
Like the leaves themselves
Turning in the wind.
Yes: but the color of the heavy hemlocks
Came striding.
And I remembered the cry of the peacocks.

The colors of their tails
Were like the leaves themselves
Turning in the wind,
In the twilight wind.
They swept over the room,
Just as they flew from the boughs of the hemlocks
Down to the ground.
I heard them cry—the peacocks.

黑　暗

[美]瓦莱斯·斯蒂芬斯(1879—1955)

黑夜,炉火边,

灌木丛的颜色

反复见面,

在屋子里翻转,

像树叶在风中回旋。

可是阴沉沉的铁杉的颜色

突然涌现,

我记起了孔雀的叫喊*。

孔雀尾的色彩

像风里回旋的树叶

扫过整个房间,

就像从铁杉的树枝上

飞落地面。

我听到那声音——是孔雀在叫喊。

这叫声是对黄昏的装饰,

* 孔雀的鸣叫被认为是不祥之兆。

Was it a cry against the twilight
Or against the leaves themselves
Turning in the wind,
Turning as the flames
Turned in the fire,
Turning as the tails of the peacocks
Turned in the loud fire,
Loud as the hemlocks
Full of the cry of the peacocks?
Or was it a cry against the hemlocks?

Out of the window,
I saw how the planets gathered
Like the leaves themselves
Turning in the wind.
I saw how the night came,
Came striding like the color of the heavy hemlocks.
I felt afraid.
And I remembered the cry of the peacocks.

还是陪衬这树叶在风里的回旋?

树叶翻飞像火焰,

又像那孔雀尾

在噼啪作响的火中翩跹,

这响声像那铁杉

充溢着孔雀的叫喊。

也许这叫声

正是要反抗那铁杉?

窗子外,

我看见群星汇聚,

像树叶在风里回旋,

我看见夜幕降临,

一下子笼罩大地

颜色像阴沉沉的铁杉。

我心惊,我害怕,

我记起孔雀的叫喊。

The Tree

Ezra Pound

I stood still and was a tree amid the wood,

Knowing the truth of things unseen before;

Of Daphne and the laurel bow

And that god-feasting couple old

That grew elm-oak amid the wold.

'Twas not until the gods had been

Kindly entreated, and been brought within

Unto the hearth of their heart's home

That they might do this wonder thing;

Nathless I have been a tree amid the wood

And many a new thing understood

That was rank folly to my head before.

树

［美］艾兹拉·庞德（1885—1972）

我是一棵树，静立森林中，

知道的故事许许多，以前却被人忽略：

达佛涅怎么变成了月桂树[①]，

还有那招待天神的老夫妇[②]。

老夫妇家在荒原住，

栽种榆树和橡树。

有一次天神化成路人从此过，

老夫妇殷勤款待，

融融暖意充满了小茅屋，

功德无量，神赐寿与福。

我是一棵树，静立森林中，

许多新事儿弄明白，

以前只当活见鬼！

① 达佛涅，希腊神话中的神女，因阿波罗追求不舍，向众神求助，众神（一说其父珀纽斯）把她变成了月桂树。

② 包喀斯和菲勒蒙，居住在佛律癸亚的一对老夫妇，因招待天神而被赐长寿，死后变成柞树和椴树。

In a Station of the Metro

Ezra Pound

The apparition of these faces in the crowd;

Petals on a wet, black bough.

在地铁站 *

[美]艾兹拉·庞德

人头攒动,幻影幢幢,

湿漉漉的黑枝上,花瓣儿绽放。

*《在地铁站》,意象派的经典之作。作者说它是“一刹那思想和感情的复合体”。

The Waking

扫码听诗

Theodore Roethke

I wake to sleep, and take my waking slow.

I feel my fate in what I cannot fear.

I learn by going where I have to go.

We think by feeling. What is there to know?

I hear my being dance from ear to ear.

I wake to sleep, and take my waking slow.

Of those so close beside me, which are you?

God bless the Ground! I shall walk softly there,

And learn by going where I have to go.

醒

[美]西奥多·罗斯克(1908—1963)

醒来又睡去,醒来慢悠悠,

天意既如此,何惧又何愁!

去那命中的归宿,学会怎样走。

思想靠感觉,何事须知晓?

我听见灵魂的喧呶。

醒来又睡去,醒来慢悠悠。

身边是何人,离我这样近?

上帝保佑大地!我将平静离开。

去那命中的归宿,学会怎样走。

Light takes the Tree; but who can tell us how?

The lowly worm climbs up a winding stair;

I wake to sleep, and take my waking slow.

Great Nature has another thing to do

To you and me; so take the lively air,

And, lovely, learn by going where to go.

This shaking keeps me steady. I should know.

What falls away is always. And is near.

I wake to sleep, and take my waking slow.

I learn by going where I have to go.

阳光理解树木,哪个知道缘由?

盘旋阶梯上,有蠕虫爬行,不停留。

醒来又睡去,醒来慢悠悠。

对你我,大自然还有别的事要做,

生活中除了轻松快活复何求?

去那命中的归宿,学会怎样走。

我知道,这次震动让我清醒,

该走的无法挽留,已经到了时候。

醒来又睡去,醒来慢悠悠,

去那命中的归宿,学会怎样走。

Root Cellar

Theodore Roethke

Nothing would sleep in that cellar, dank as a ditch,

Bulbs broke out of boxes hunting for chinks in the dark,

Shoots dangled and drooped,

Lolling obscenely from mildewed crates,

Hung down long yellow evil necks, like tropical snakes.

And what a congress of stinks!

Roots ripe as old bait,

Pulpy stems, rank, silo-rich,

Leaf-mold, manure, lime, piled against slippery planks.

Nothing would give up life:

Even the dirt kept breathing a small breath.

根 窖

[美]西奥多·罗斯克(1908—1963)

那地窖像阴沟一样潮湿，

谁也不肯在那里逗留。

鳞茎爆开，黑暗中从箱子里寻隙探头，

低垂的枝条晃悠悠，

从发霉的柳条箱里，荡下黄色的脖颈，

像热带的蛇，令人作呕。

好一个污秽杂物的大聚首！

成熟的根是古老的诱惑，

多汁的茎秆茁壮而馥郁。

滑腻腻的木板旁，是一堆堆粪肥、石灰、腐叶土。

一切的一切都不肯放弃生命，

连泥土都在轻声地呼吸。

When Serpents Bargain for the Right to Squirm

e. e. cummings*

When serpents bargain for the right to squirm
and the sun strikes to gain a living wage—
when thorns regard their roses with alarm
and rainbows are insured against old age

when every thrush may sing no new moon in
if all screech-owls have not okeyed his voice
—and any wave signs on the dotted line
or else an ocean is compelled to close

when the oak begs permission of the birch
to make an acorn—valleys accuse their
mountains of having altitude—and march
denounces april as a saboteur

then we'll believe in that incredible
unanimal mankind (and not until).

* 卡明斯有独特的书写规则。诗行开头与月份名称都不用大写,连自己的姓名也不用大写。

啥时候蛇要谈判蠕动权

［美］卡明斯（1894—1962）

啥时候蛇要谈判蠕动权，

太阳罢了工，谋生去赚钱，

棘刺盯着它们的玫瑰，一脸惊恐，

彩虹上了保险，不许老人看。

啥时候，并非每只鸫都能唱得新月升，

并非每只叫枭都说鸫的歌好听；

一波波的浪头都要签字画押，

不然大海就要关闭，停止汹涌。

啥时候橡树结果

须得白桦的认同，

山谷控告大山的高耸，

三月谴责四月捣乱的罪行。

到那时，我们才能相信

那不可依赖的非兽人类（此前不行）。

The Wind

James Stevens

The wind stood up and gave a shout.

He whistled on his fingers and

Kicked the withered leaves about

And thumped the branches with his hand

And said he'd kill and kill and kill

And so he will and so he will.

风

[爱尔兰]詹姆斯·斯蒂芬斯(1882—1950)

风刮起,发出一阵喧哗,

夹着凄厉的口哨声,萧萧,飒飒。

把枯枝败叶狂扫,

把青枝绿叶鞭打。

嚷叫着:它要杀杀,它要飒飒,

是的,它定会杀杀,它定会飒飒。

The Taxi

Amy Lowell

When I go away from you

The world beats dead

Like a slackened drum.

I call out for you against the jutted stars

And shout into the ridges of the wind.

Streets coming fast,

One after the other,

Wedge you away from me,

And the lamps of the city prick my eyes

So that I can no longer see your face.

Why should I leave you,

To wound myself upon the sharp edges of the night?

出租车

[美]艾米·洛威尔(1874—1925)

当我从你的身边走开,

这世界像松弛的鼓,

变得没精打采。

我呼叫你,对着这无边的星空,

声音融进了那呼啸的风。

一条又一条街道,

从我眼前闪过,

越来越大的距离隔开了你我。

城市的灯光扎眼,

我再也看不清你的容颜。

为什么我要离开你,正此时:

天将明,夜阑珊?

$E = mc^2$

Morris Bishop

What was our trust, we trust not,

What was our faith, we doubt;

Whether we must or must not

We may debate about.

The soul perhaps is a gust of gas.

And wrong is a form of right—

But we know that Energy equals Mass

By the Square of the Speed of Light.

What we have known, we know not,

What we have proved, abjure.

Life is a tangled bow-knot,

But one thing still is sure.

Come, little lad; come, little lass,

Your docile creed recite:

“We know that Energy equals Mass

By the Square of the Speed of light.”

$E=mc^2$

[美]莫里斯·毕绍普(1893—1973)

我们相信的,我们又怀疑,
我们信仰的,其实并不信仰。
不管是必须的,还是严禁的,
我们都拿来辩论一场。
灵魂也许就是一股子气,
谬误不过是正确的另一个模样。
但我们确实知道
能量等于物质乘以光速的平方。

我们已知的,其实并不知,
我们确证的,又弃之一旁。
生活就是一团乱麻,
只有一件事确凿无疑。
来,来,小伙子,小姑娘,
背会你们最简单的信条:
"能量等于物质乘以光速的平方。"

Night of Spring

Thomas Westwood

Slow, horses, slow,

As through the wood we go—

We would count the stars in heaven,

Hear the grasses grow:

Watch the cloudlets few

Dappling the deep blue,

In our open palms outspread

Catch the blessed dew.

Slow, horses, slow,

As through the wood we go—

春　夜

[美]韦斯特伍德(1814—1888)

慢慢走,马儿,慢慢走,

陪我且向林中游。

去数一数天上的星星,

倾听小草的生长声,青青。

看那几小片云块,

斑驳了那天宇的蔚蓝。

伸开手掌,

去捕捉那祈福的露珠。

慢慢走,马儿,慢慢走,

陪我且向林中游。

We would see fair Dian rise
With her huntress bow:

We would hear the breeze
Ruffling the dim trees,
Hear its sweet love-ditty set
To endless harmonies.

Slow, horses, slow,
As through the wood we go—
All the beauty of the night
We would learn and know!

看猎户星升起在天穹，

还佩着她打猎的弓。

听一阵微风吹过，

扰动那幽幽树梢如波。

那甜美的音涛，

汹涌成无尽的歌谣。

慢慢走,马儿,慢慢走，

陪我且向林中游。

这春夜的美与醉，

陪我尽情地阅览享受。

Mid-August at Sourdough Mountain Lookout

Gary Snyder

扫码听诗

Down valley a smoke haze

Three days heat, after five days rain

Pitch glows on the fir-cones

Across rocks and meadows

Swarms of new flies.

I cannot remember things I once read

A few friends, but they are in cities.

Drinking cold snow-water from a tin cup

Looking down for miles

Through high still air.

八月中旬索豆山守望台

［美］斯奈德（1930—　）

山谷里升起朦胧的雾霭，

五天连阴雨，三天暑气蒸腾，

冷杉的球果上，树脂亮晶晶。

嶙峋的岩石和草地上，

新生的蝇群闹营营。

读过的东西都已忘，

有过几个朋友，住在城厢，

铁皮杯里雪水冰凉。

透过高旷而凝滞的空气，

我眺望山下朦胧的远方。

Nantucket

William Carlos Williams

Flowers through the window

lavender and yellow

changes by white curtains—

Smell of cleanliness—

Sunshine of late afternoon—

On the glass tray

a glass pitcher, the tumbler

turned down, by which

a key is lying—And the

immaculate white bed

南塔基特岛

[美]威廉斯(1883—1963)

透过窗看见那花儿

淡紫,金黄;

雪白的窗帘轻晃,

把小屋变成色彩的交响。

净无尘,溢芬芳。

近黄昏,

玻璃盘上日色曛。

水罐静坐,酒杯倒扣。

一把钥匙陪在旁,

洁白无瑕的床铺细端详。

第三辑 爱在迷人的春天

Siren Song

Margaret Atwood

扫 码 听 诗

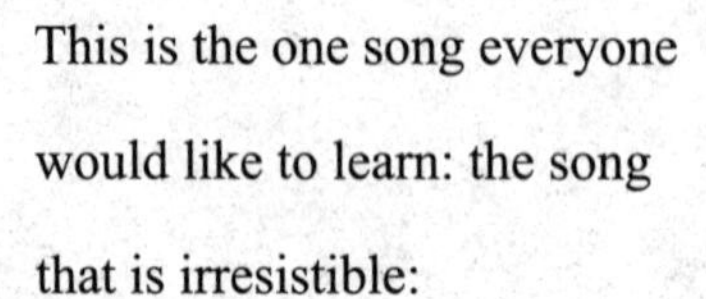

This is the one song everyone
would like to learn: the song
that is irresistible:

the song that forces men
to leap overboard in squadrons
even though they see beached skulls
the song nobody knows
because anyone who had heard it
is dead, and the others can’t remember.

Shall I tell you the secret
and if I do, will you get me
out of this bird suit?

海妖塞壬*之歌

[加拿大]玛格丽特·阿特伍德(1939—　)

这歌儿人人都想学，

它的声音能迷住人的魂魄：

船上的水手

一个个朝海里跳，

也不管有多少骷髅飘上那小岛。

没有人知道那歌曲，

听见的人全都去了天国，

别的人也早已把它忘却。

我想把这秘密告诉你，

你能不能帮我

把这一身鸟羽脱掉？

* 塞壬，半人半鸟的水妖，居海岛，用迷人的歌声诱惑航海者，使他们成为海妖们的牺牲品。奥德赛（即尤利西斯）用蜡封住同伴的耳朵，并叫人把自己绑在桅杆上，从而脱险。

I don't enjoy it here
squatting on this island
looking picturesque and mythical

with these two feathery maniacs,
I don't enjoy singing
this trio, fatal and valuable.

I will tell the secret to you,
to you, only to you.
Come closer. This song

is a cry for help: Help me!
Only you, only you can,
you are unique

at last. Alas
it is a boring song
but it works every time.

蜗居在这岛上

我并不快乐，

尽管它景色如画，美丽而又神秘。

同两个鸟怪搭在一起，

搞那三重唱我并不乐意，

那歌曲听了要送命，虽然它珍贵无比。

我要把这秘密告诉你，

单单告诉你

走近点。这歌儿是

救命！——一支呼救曲。

只有你非比寻常，

只有你当得起。

哎，还有，

这歌儿的确单调，

可是它回回都能奏效。

A White Rose

John Boyle O'Reilly

扫码听诗

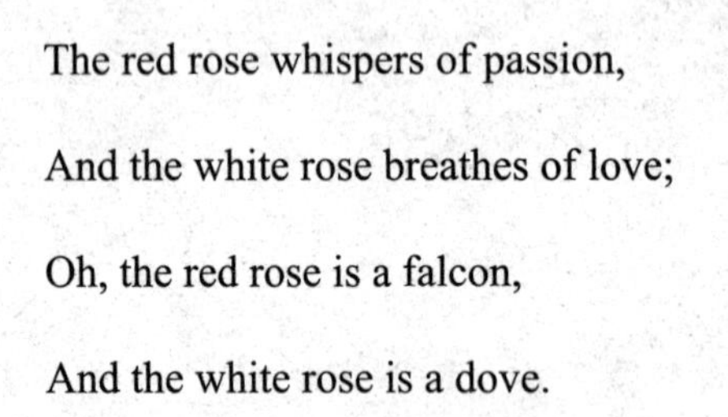

The red rose whispers of passion,

And the white rose breathes of love;

Oh, the red rose is a falcon,

And the white rose is a dove.

But I send you a cream-white rosebud,

With a flush on its petal tips;

For the love that is purest and sweetest

Has a kiss of desire on the lips.

白玫瑰

[爱尔兰]约翰·波伊尔·欧莱里(1844—1890)

白玫瑰悄声谈论爱的纯洁,

红玫瑰窃窃私语爱的激情。

哦,白玫瑰是鸽子,

红玫瑰是猎鹰。

我给你寄去乳白色的玫瑰花蕾,

花瓣尖上晕出一点绯红。

唇上渴望的真情的吻,

正是纯洁甜蜜的爱的象征。

Love Is a Sickness

Samuel Daniel

Love is a sickness full of woes,

All remedies refusing;

A plant that with most cutting grows,

Most barren with best using.

Why so?

More we enjoy it, more it dies;

If not enjoy'd, it sighing cries—

Heigh ho!

爱是一种疾病

［英］丹尼尔（1562—1619）

爱是一种疾病，痛苦充满心胸，

什么药方都不灵。

爱像一种植物，越修剪越茁壮，

呵护备至反而凋零。

为何？

爱之泉经不起醉饮，醉饮无度它就干涸。

不迷不醉，让它一声叹息拂过，

呃嗬！

To Celia

扫 码 听 诗

Ben Jonson

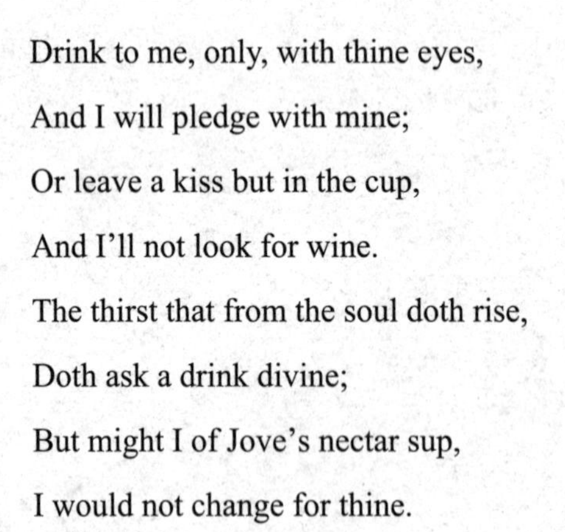

Drink to me, only, with thine eyes,
And I will pledge with mine;
Or leave a kiss but in the cup,
And I'll not look for wine.
The thirst that from the soul doth rise,
Doth ask a drink divine;
But might I of Jove's nectar sup,
I would not change for thine.

I sent thee, late, a rosy wreath,
Not so much honouring thee,
As giving it a hope, that there
It could not withered be.
But thou thereon did'st only breathe,
And sent'st it back to me,
Since when it grows, and smells, I swear,
Not of itself, but thee.

致西里亚

［英］本·琼森（1572—1637）

为我祝酒吧，哪怕只用你的眼波，

我会信守我的承诺。

或者在杯中留下深情的吻，

空杯也能解我的饥渴。

这是心灵深处的意愿，

给我神仙的琼浆也不肯交换。

送你一个玫瑰的花环，

在你身旁它会永远鲜艳。

当花里融进你的气息，

再让它回到我的身边。

从此，你的芬芳，

将与我终生相伴。

To Celia

Ben Jonson

Come my Celia, let us prove,

While we may, the sports of love;

Time will not be ours forever;

He at length our good will sever.

Spend not then his gifts in vain.

Suns that set may rise again;

But if once we lose this light,

'Tis with us perpetual night.

Why should we defer our joys?

Fame and rumour are but toys.

Cannot we delude the eyes

Of a few poor household spies,

Or his easier ears beguile,

So removed by our wile?

'Tis no sin love's fruit to steal;

But the sweet thefts to reveal,

To be taken, to be seen,

These have crimes accounted been.

致西里亚

[英]本·琼森

来,西里亚,让我们探讨,

什么是爱的真谛。

时光不会永远属于我们,

美好的愿望到头来都会抛弃。

不要枉然浪费了上苍的馈赠,

太阳落山还会升起,

要是一旦失去了阳光,

伴随我们的将是

永恒的黑暗,荆天棘地。

为何把我们的欢乐推到将来?

名望与谣诼都不过是一种玩具。

难道能瞒住几个"密探"的耳目,

即使是我们施了巧计?

偷食爱情之果算不了什么罪恶,

可要揭露"窃蜜",让它暴露于光天化日,

人们倒说是一种罪戾。

Sonnet 75

Edmund Spenser

One day I wrote her name upon the strand,

But came the waves and washed it away:

Again I wrote it with a second hand,

But came the tide and made my pains his prey.

"Vain man," said she, "that doest in vain assay.

A mortal thing so to immortalize,

For I myself shall like to this decay,

And eek my name be wiped out likewise."

"Not so," quod I, "let baser things devise,

To die in dust,but you shall live by fame:

My verse your virtues rare shall eternize,

And in the heavens write your glorious name.

Where whenas death shall all the world subdue,

Our love shall live, and later life renew."

十四行诗(75)

[英]埃德蒙·斯宾塞(1552—1599)

海滩上,我写下她的芳名,

拍岸的波涛把它冲得干干净净。

换手再写,

汹涌的潮水把我的苦心化成泡影。

“高傲的人啊,”她说,“你想让速朽的事物永恒,

终究会徒劳无功。

我情愿这样一天天衰朽,

连同我的名字一起消泯。”

“不,”我说,“凡夫俗子用尽心机总归尘土,

你将活着,伴随着你的声名。

我的诗歌会把你的美德永远传播,

你光荣的名字将列入天堂的群英。

死神纵然会让全世界臣服,

但我们的爱情长存,让后世的生活复兴。”

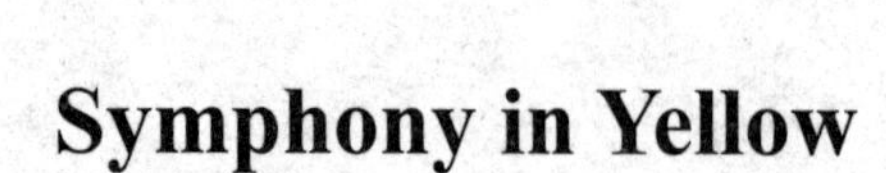

Symphony in Yellow

Oscar Wilde

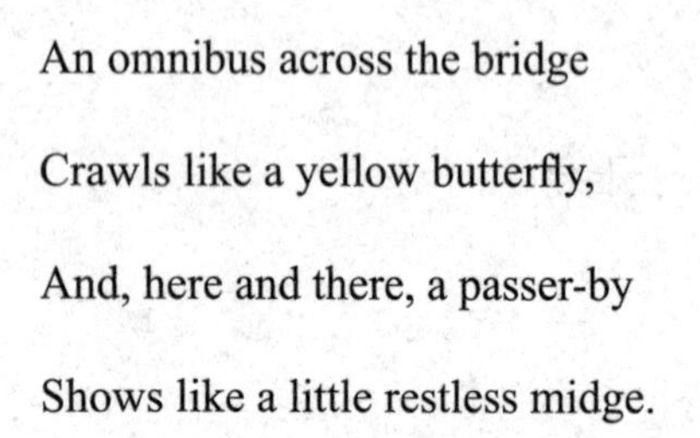

An omnibus across the bridge

Crawls like a yellow butterfly,

And, here and there, a passer-by

Shows like a little restless midge.

Big barges full of yellow hay

Are moored against the shadowy wharf,

And, like a yellow silken scarf,

The thick fog hangs along the quay.

The yellow leaves begin to fade

And flutter from the temple elms,

And at my feet the pale green Thames

Lies like a rod of rippled jade.

黄的交响

［爱尔兰］奥斯卡·王尔德（1854—1900）

一辆车从桥上穿越，

蠕动着，像嫩黄的蝴蝶。

零零落落的行人，

像永不停歇的小虫飞过。

驳船上装满了金黄的干草，

在多荫的码头停泊。

浓雾飘拂，

像鹅黄的丝巾，把河岸包裹。

苍黄的树叶开始凋谢，

从教堂的榆树上纷纷飘落。

像涟漪浮动的玉带，

泰晤士河从我脚下流过。

Virtue

George Herbert

扫码听诗

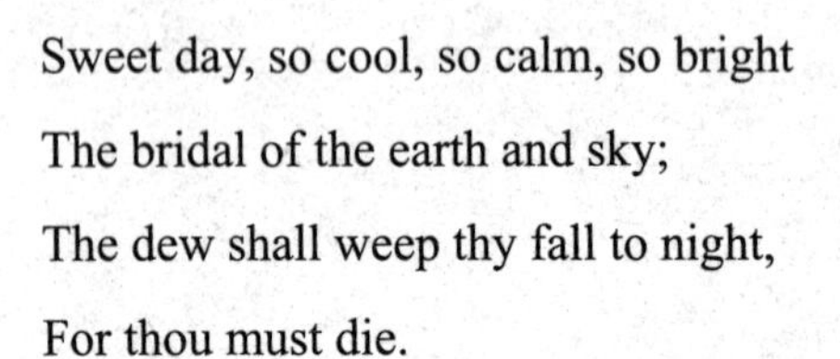

Sweet day, so cool, so calm, so bright
The bridal of the earth and sky;
The dew shall weep thy fall to night,
For thou must die.

Sweet rose, whose hue, angry and brave,
Bids the rash gazer wipe his eyes;
Thy root is ever in its grave,
And thou must die.

Sweet spring, full of sweet days and roses,
A box where sweets compacted lie;
My music shows ye have your closes,
And all must die.

Only a sweet and virtuous soul,
Like seasoned timber, never gives;
But though the whole world turn to coal.
Then chiefly lives.

德　行

［英］乔治·赫伯特（1593—1633）

白昼多美好，明丽又安详，
你是大地与天空的拜堂；
露珠晶莹为你哭，
黑夜降临，你将消亡。

玫瑰多美好，热烈又芬芳，
引人凝眸擦眼来观赏。
可叹根就在自己的坟里，
季候一到，你将凋伤。

春天多美好，有白昼的明丽，玫瑰的芬芳，
像一个装满了宇宙精华的百宝箱。
可惜流水落花春去也，
万物繁华都有收场。

只有崇高美好的灵魂不会消逝，
像防腐的原木永不断裂。
待世界变成煤炭，
它仍旧活着，带着能量。

A Child's Laughter

Algernon Charles Swinburne

All the bells of heaven may ring,

All the birds of heaven may sing,

All the bells on earth may spring,

All the winds on earth may bring

  All sweet sounds together;

Sweeter far than all things heard,

Hand of harper, tone of bird,

Sound of woods at sundawn stirred,

Welling water's winsome word,

  Wind in warm wan weather,

One thing yet there is, that none

Hearing ere its chime be done

Knows not well the sweetest one

Heard of man beneath the sun,

  Hoped in heaven hereafter;

孩子的笑

［英］斯温伯恩（1837—1909）

让天堂里所有的铃铎敲响，百鸟齐鸣，

让地上万钟振动，清风聚拢一切的天籁清音：

鸟鸣喈喈，竖琴铮铮，

黄昏时分的阵阵林涛，

涓涓泉水喜洋洋的喷涌，

还有那郁闷的日子里呼啸的暖风；

比起这一切

有一种曲调更动听；

不必等曲终人散，你就会知道

这是太阳底下

人们听到的最甜美的声音，

是日后天堂里的憧憬：

Soft and strong and loud and light,

Very sound of very light

Heard from morning's rosiest height,

When the soul of all delight

Fills a child's clear laughter.

Golden bells of welcome rolled

Never forth such notes, nor told

Hours so blithe in tones so bold,

As the radiant mouth of gold

Here that rings forth heaven.

If the golden-crested wren

Were a nightingale—why, then,

Something seen and heard of men

Might be half as sweet as when

Laughs a child of seven.

柔和,刚劲,响亮,轻松,

正是那晨光辉煌时刻的声响和光景,

当无比欢乐的灵魂

涌进那孩子爽朗的笑声。

迎宾的金钟从未发出过如此美妙的旋律,

也从未用这样豪勇的音调报告喜庆;

那孩子真情洋溢的嘴里发出的笑,

回响着天堂圣乐之声。

人们也许听说过

金色羽冠的鹪鹩变成了夜莺,

逸闻美谈使人感动,

远不如七岁孩子灿烂的笑容。

Spring, the Sweet Spring

Thomas Nashe

Spring, the sweet spring, is the year's pleasant king,

Then blooms each thing, then maids dance in a ring,

Cold doth not sting, the pretty birds do sing:

Cuckoo, jug-jug, pu-we, to-witta-woo!

The palm and may make country houses gay,

Lambs frisk and play, the shepherds pipe all day,

And we hear aye birds tune this merry lay:

Cuckoo, jug-jug, pu-we, to-witta-woo!

The fields breathe sweet, the daisies kiss our feet,

Young lovers meet, old wives a-sunning sit,

In every street these tunes our ears do greet:

Cuckoo, jug-jug, pu-we, to witta-woo!

Spring，the sweet spring！

迷人的春天

[英]托马斯·纳什(1567—1601)

迷人的春天,欢乐的精灵,

花儿绽放,少女舞翩翩。

冲破清寒,鸟儿的歌声飞向云天:

谷谷——恰恰——喈喈——关关。

绿树婆娑,掩映着村舍里笑语一片,

羊羔撒欢儿,牧人衔着烟斗,悠闲。

耳边传来鸟儿的千种鸣啭:

谷谷——恰恰——喈喈——关关。

田野散发着芬芳,雏菊开在你脚边。

年轻恋人来幽会,老婆子们晒太阳取暖。

大街小巷回荡着鸟儿的谣曲:

谷谷——恰恰——喈喈——关关。

春天,迷人的春天!

第四辑

太阳落山

Spring and Fall—*To a Young Child*

Gerard Manley Hopkins

扫 码 听 诗

Margaret, are you grieving

Over Golden grove unleaving?

Leaves, like the things of man, you

With your fresh thoughts care for, can you?

Ah! as the heart grows older

It will come to such sights colder

By and by, nor spare a sigh

Though worlds of wanwood leafmeal lie;

And yet you will weep and know why.

Now no matter, child, the name:

Sorrow's springs are the same.

Nor mouth had, no nor mind, expressed

What heart heard of, ghost guessed:

It is the blight man was born for,

It is Margaret you mourn for.

春与秋——写给一个孩子

[英]杰拉尔德·曼利·霍普金斯(1844—1889)

看到金色的树林叶枯叶落，

玛格丽特,你有没有感到悲伤?

思想清新的你,肯不肯珍惜这些落叶，

像珍惜你的用品一样?

啊,心随人变老,渐渐地

你会冷漠地看待这些景象，

匆匆走过,没有叹息和惆怅，

尽管是遍地黄叶,一片苍凉。

可是你终将痛哭失声,懂得世事沧桑。

孩子,叫啥名字并不重要，

恼人的春天也是这般模样。

小鬼不是没头脑，

只是没有说出心灵听到的声响：

人一出生就奔向衰老，

玛格丽特才是你的哀伤。

The Sun Has Set

Emily Brontë

The sun has set, and the long grass now

Waves dreamily in the evening wind;

And the wild bird has flown from that old gray stone

In some warm nook a couch to find.

In all the lonely landscape round

I see no light and hear no sound,

Except the wind that far away

Come sighing o'er the heathy sea.

太阳落山

［英］艾米莉·勃朗特（1818—1848）

太阳落到山的后面，

草棵在晚风中摇曳，恍如梦幻；

野鸟飞起，离开了旧居灰岩，

找个温暖的角落把新巢建。

周围是一片死寂的景物，

没有亮光，没有声响，

只有风在远处呜咽，

一声声回荡在石南丛生的荒原。

When I Came Last to Ludlow

Alfred Edward Housman

扫 码 听 诗

When I came last to Ludlow

Amides the moonlight pale,

Two friends kept step beside me,

Two honest lads and hale.

Now Dick lies long in the churchyard,

And Ned lies long in jail,

And I came home to Ludlow

Amidst the moonlight pale.

我上次回到拉德洛

[英]阿尔弗雷德·爱德华·豪斯曼(1859—1936)

当我上次回到拉德洛的故乡，

一路上沐浴着淡淡的月光，

身边有好友两个，

小伙子诚实又健壮。

如今，狄克已长眠在教堂的墓园，

奈德却安居在牢房。

我又一次回到拉德洛的故乡，

一路上沐浴着淡淡的月光。

There Was a Young Lady of Riga

Anonymous

扫 码 听 诗

There was a young lady of Riga

Who went for a ride on tiger;

They returned from the ride

With the lady inside,

And a smile on the face of the tiger.

有个少妇叫丽嘉

佚名

有个少妇叫丽嘉，

她竟敢骑虎走天下，

旅游归来他们俩，

虎腹里的少妇没说啥，

一丝微笑虎脸上挂。

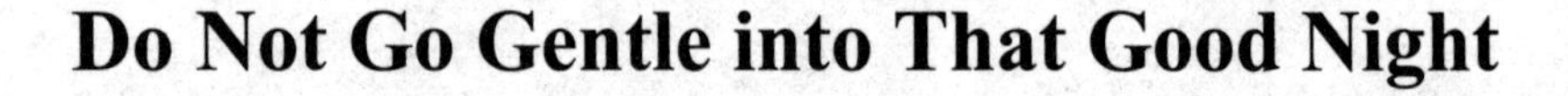

Do Not Go Gentle into That Good Night

Dylan Thomas

扫码听诗

Do not go gentle into that good night,

Old age should burn and rave at close of day;

Rage, rage against the dying of the light.

Though wise men at their end know dark is right,

Because their words had forked no lightning they

Do not go gentle into that good night.

Good men, the last wave by, crying how bright

Their frail deeds might have danced in a green bay,

Rage, rage against the dying of the light.

不要乖乖地走进那黑夜之邦

［英］迪伦·托马斯(1914—1953)

不要乖乖地走进那黑夜之邦，

人到暮年也要燃起生活的渴望，

怒吼，抗争，决不熄灭生命的火光。

聪明人虽知道夜是常态，

他们的话语不会像电火闪亮，

谁也不肯走进那黑夜之邦。

善良的人们最后告别，发出最后的呼喊——

他们微末的德行将辉映在绿色的港湾上，

怒吼，抗争，决不熄灭生命的火光。

Wild men who caught and sang the sun in flight,

And learn, too late, they grieved it on its way,

Do not go gentle into that good night.

Grave men, near death, who see with blinding sight

Blind eyes could blaze like meteors and be gay,

Rage, rage against the dying of the light.

And you, my father, there on that sad height,

Curse, bless, me now with your fierce tears, I pray.

Do not go gentle into that good night.

Rage, rage against the dying of the light.

大胆的人们飞天追星颂太阳，

到后来才知道半路上会生出忧伤，

不，不要乖乖地走进那黑夜之邦。

严肃的人们临终欣然，看世事豁然开朗，

目眇眇如流星一闪，

怒吼，抗争，决不熄灭生命的火光。

您，父亲，沉浸在痛苦的深渊里，

咒骂我吧，祝福我吧，用你的热泪沾裳。

不要乖乖走进那黑夜之邦，

怒吼，抗争，决不熄灭生命的火光。

She, at His Funeral

Thomas Hardy

They bear him to his resting-place—

In slow procession sweeping by;

I follow at a stranger's space;

His kindred they, his sweetheart I.

Unchanged my gown of garish dye,

Though sable-sad is their attire;

But they stand round with griefless eye,

Whilst my regret consumes like fire!

送葬

［英］托马斯·哈代（1840—1928）

他们送他到安息的地方，

缓缓地走过，长长的一行，

我跟在看客的群里，为他送葬。

他们是他的亲属，我是他的心上人。

他们穿着乌黑的丧服，

我却没有换去华裳。

但他们冷漠地站着，眼里没有哀伤，

我心里燃起的痛苦，像火一样。

The House on the Hill

扫 码 听 诗

Edwin Arlington Robinson

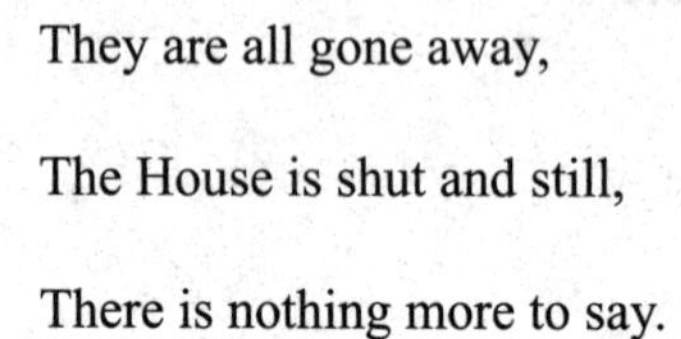

They are all gone away,

The House is shut and still,

There is nothing more to say.

Through broken walls and gray

The winds blow bleak and shrill.

They are all gone away.

Nor is there one to-day

To speak them good or ill:

There is nothing more to say.

山上的房子

［美］罗宾逊（1869—1935）

他们都已离开，

关门闭户，死样的寂寥，

别的再也无言相告。

透过灰色的残垣，

风在凄厉地呼啸。

他们都已离开。

如今没有人

对他们说三道四：

别的再也无言相告。

Why is it then we stray

Around the sunken sill?

They are all gone away.

And our poor fancy-play

For them is wasted skill:

There is nothing more to say.

There is ruin and decay

In the House on the Hill:

They are all gone away,

There is nothing more to say.

既如此,为何我们还流连徘徊

绕着这沉降的窗台?

他们都已离开。

我们那可怜的想象力

对他们是滥用的技巧:

别的再也无言相告。

山上的房子里

只剩下废墟和破败:

他们都已离开。

别的再也无言相告。

After Long Silence

William Butler Yeats

Speech after long silence; it is right,

All other lovers being estranged or dead,

Unfriendly lamplight hid under its shade,

The curtains drawn upon unfriendly night,

That we descant and yet again descant

Upon the supreme theme of Art and Song:

Bodily decrepitude is wisdom; young

We loved each other and were ignorant.

长久的沉默以后

［爱尔兰］叶芝

长久的沉默憋出一句话。这也难怪，

既然别的爱侣都已疏远，或者羽化，

冷漠的夜晚挡在窗帘外，

不祥的灯火躲在灯罩下，

我们就只好反复谈论那崇高的课题，

美术或歌曲之类的闲话：

躯体的衰老是一种智慧，年轻时

我们毕竟相爱过，虽然那时不懂啥。

译后记

本书81首诗歌的原文,主要从下列英语诗歌理论研究著作和文学评论著作中选出。这些著作所提供的作者生平以及写作背景等材料,对译者的理解甚有裨益,谨向编著者表示由衷的谢意。

1. *Poetry in English*《英语诗歌》(高广文编著,西安交通大学出版社,2010)

2. *The Introduction to English Poetry*《英语诗歌导读》(张金霞主编,河北大学出版社,2008)

3. *British and American Poetry: A Guide to Its Understanding* and *Appreciation*《英美诗歌鉴赏》(黄家修主编,武汉大学出版社,2009)

4. *A Course of English Poetry*《英国诗歌教程》(戴继国编著,对外经济贸易大学出版社,2005)

5. *A Survey of English Poetry*《英诗概论》(罗良功编著,武汉大学出版社,2002)

6. *Appreciation of Famous British and American Poetry*《英美诗歌名篇赏析》(逯阳主编,大连理工大学出版社,2013)

7. *Selected Readings in American Poetry*《美国诗歌选读》(陶洁主编,北京大学出版社,2008)

8. *Selected Canons of British and American Poetry*《英诗鉴赏入门》(王勇,龙江编著,武汉大学出版社,2009)

附 录

生命的密码（代自传）

问余何事常欣欣，

漫走闲坐有柳荫。

今世幸知养猪乐，

他生再作牧马人。

钢板钻穿三千尺，

字母生吞两万斤。

呼啸山庄[1]风呼啸，

埃敦荒原[2]雨倾盆。

老来更知书读少，

① Emily Brontë，*Wuthering Heights*（《呼啸山庄》故事的背景地）.

② Thomas Hardy，*The Return of the Native*（《还乡》故事的背景地）.

青春未识大学门。

踟躇前行路漫漫，

求索难煞独眼人。

雪意凄其怀秋白[③]，

心事寂寥读鲁迅。

梦魂常系伏尔加[④]，

何日西游去牛津？

写罢不知何处寄，

暮色苍茫掩柴门。

③ 瞿秋白赠鲁迅诗："雪意凄其心惘然，江南旧梦已如烟。天寒沽酒长安市，犹折梅花伴醉眠。"

④ 俄罗斯大河。